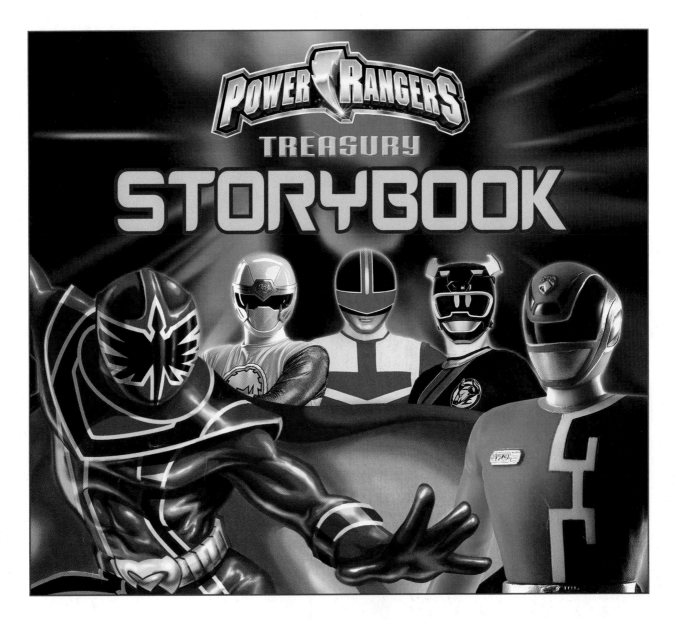

Adapted by Kathryn Knight
Designed by Andy Mangrum

ISBN: 1-40372-349-4 (X) 1-40372-918-2 (M)

Dalmatian Press, LLC, 2006. All rights reserved. Printed in Canada. The DALMATIAN PRESS name and logo are trademarks of Dalmatian Press, LLC, Franklin, Tennessee 37067.
No part of this book may be reproduced or copied in any form without written permission of Dalmatian Press, BVS Entertainment, Inc., and BVS International N.V.

06 07 08 09 TRN 10 9 8 7 6 5 4 3 2 1 — 15389 POWER RANGERS - Treasury Storybook

TABLE OF CONTENTS

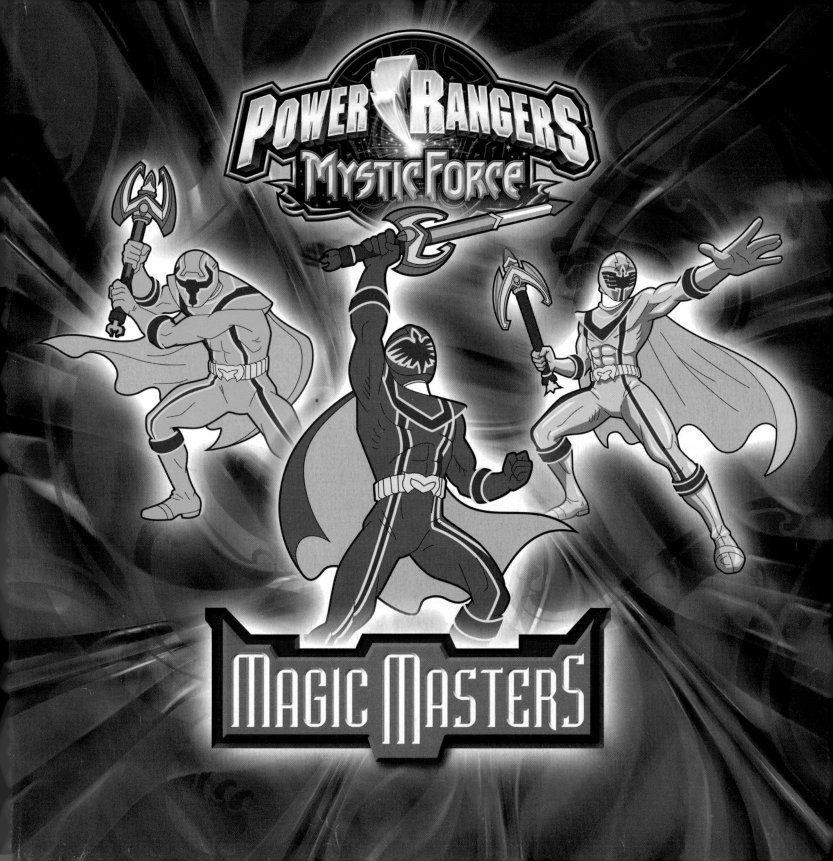

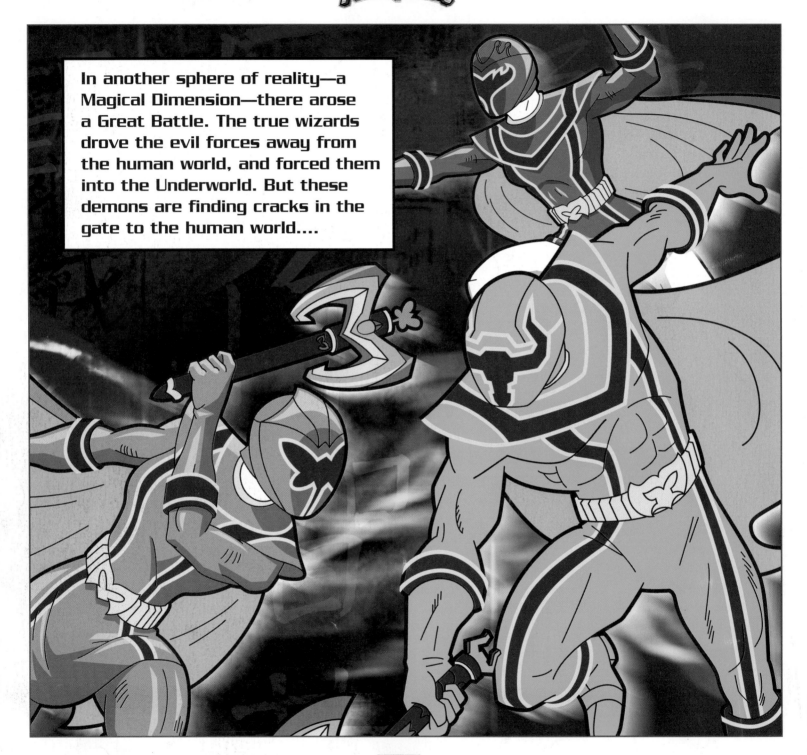

In another sphere of reality—a Magical Dimension—there arose a Great Battle. The true wizards drove the evil forces away from the human world, and forced them into the Underworld. But these demons are finding cracks in the gate to the human world....

Udonna, the sorceress, has chosen five brave teens to fight the evil demons. These mystical warriors are the Mystic Force Power Rangers!

Xander is the Green Mystic Ranger, of great agility and strength. The elements of earth become his weapons.

Vida is the Pink Mystic Ranger, sister to Madison. She is a shape-shifter with the power of wind and air.

Chip is the Yellow Mystic Ranger, who can control light and electricity.

With the call of *Galwit Mysto Aerotan*, their magical brooms became powerful Mystic Racers, transporting them to the scene of the crime!

"I think we could reason with this Knight Wolf," suggested Xander. "Think again!" responded Vida.

Suddenly, before them stood the mighty Koragg— the Knight Wolf.

"Darkness has come!" he roared. "Prove to me your worthiness, Rangers! Hidiacs, arise!"

At Koragg's command, an army of zombies arose from the Underworld!

With the powers of nature, the five Mystic Rangers battled and destroyed the Hidiacs!

"How'd you like *that* heat, Koragg?" taunted Nick.

"Great job!" said Nick.

"We better report back to Udonna at Rootcore," said Chip.

"Yeah," added Madison. "After all, we know we'll be seeing him again...."

"Right! And next time, I'm going to reason with him!" announced Xander.

Vida gave him a sideways glance. "Ya think?"

Fifteen years in the future, a planet-conquering alien force, led by Emperor Gruumm, has turned its destructive attention to Earth! Only the Space Patrol Delta Rangers can stop them.

Using teamwork and light-speed Zord vehicles to battle evil, they unite to become the ultimate force for good—Power Rangers S.P.D.!

Jack Landers is the Red S.P.D. Ranger, the squad leader. He is able to molecularize himself and pass through solid objects.

"Sky" Tate is the Blue S.P.D. Ranger, the son of a former Red Ranger. He is able to create force fields.

Bridge Carson, a master mechanic with psychic powers, is the Green S.P.D. Ranger.

The Yellow S.P.D. Ranger is "Z" Delgado, who can clone herself.

The Pink S.P.D. Ranger is Sydney Drew—the baton wielding beauty!

Jack and Sydney must use teamwork and martial arts skills to defeat a fierce Krybot.
"Do you give up yet?" roared the Krybot.
"No way!" answered Jack.

With the defeat of the Krybot, yet another call was sent for the S.P.D. Rangers.

S.P.D. Emergency!
Morphers in Ignition Mode!

The Rangers were dispatched from Delta Base in their Squad Runners— elite emergency vehicles.

Piloted by the Rangers, the Delta Squad Runners are equipped with state-of-the-art lasers, lasso-throwing capabilities, and blasters.

Power Rangers—
to the rescue!

Meanwhile, the S.P.D. Commander, Anubis "Doggie" Cruger, had also received a summons from his old enemy, General Benaag!

"Meet me in Sector 4, Area 6, Cruger!"

"I am here, Benaag, to avenge my fallen people of Sirius whom you destroyed!" announced Doggie—though he had vowed to never pick up his sword again.

"You escaped last time, Galaxy Defender—this time you will not!"

Back in the city, a huge robot was drilling proton spikes into the ground. The next spike—a mega neutron spike—would cause an earthquake on a Quasar 3 level!

But the rangers arrived on the scene just in time to battle the drilling villain!

"Are you guys ready for this?"

"Yeah!"

"I'm in!"

"Me, too!"

"Go for it!"

"Lock 'em in, Rangers!" commanded the Red Ranger.

Delta Squad Megazord!

100 Troobian Krybots now faced the Commander.

"You defeated my people and you have taken what is dearest to me, Benaag, but that has only made me stronger. For I am..."

The Rangers were called to Sector 4, Area 6, where they saw the Shadow Ranger standing over the defeated Benaag.

"Who is that Ranger?" asked Jack. "It's—it's Commander Cruger!" they all called out in amazement.

Containment Mode!

Benaag was reduced to a mere squirming image on a Containment Card— and taken back to Command Base.

Watching the scene from his lair, Gruumm grumbled, "Yes, I have failed this time, for I have underestimated the Power Rangers."

Once again, through Discipline, Control, and Teamwork....
Justice prevails!

Deep in the mountains, secret Ninja Academies once trained young people in the Ninja arts. After the evil Lothor destroyed the schools, only three Ninjas remained, guided by their wise Ninja Master—the Sensei.

These young champions were called to defend the Earth against Lothor and his greed for power and control. They are the Ninja Storm Power Rangers.

The Sensei challenged the three teens to be guided, not just by might and strength, but by wisdom and teamwork. He equipped them with Wind Morphers, amazing tsunami cycles, and the powers of nature.

To Shane, the risk-taking skateboarder, he gave the power of air and sky. As the Red Wind Ranger, Shane calls upon wind and fire to do battle with Lothor's henchmen.

To Tori, the sensible surfer, the Sensei gave the power of water. As the Blue Wind Ranger, Tori summons thunderous waves to drown Lothor's quest for evil.

To Dustin, the carefree dirtbike racer, he gave the power of earth. As the Yellow Wind Ranger, Dustin commands rock and solid ground to bury the enemy's hopes of victory.

Lothor and his ruthless general, Zurgane, sent armies of Kelzaks and menacing monsters to take over the Earth—all to no avail. The skills and powers of this well-trained team of teens thwarted his plans every time.

The dark energy was strong in Lothor. He had once been a Ninja, so he knew the one way he could defeat this team. "Time to shake things up," he growled in his space headquarters. "And split them up!" he added with a proud laugh.

Back on Earth, the ground began to shake. Buildings cracked, huge boulders rolled, and people fled in terror. The source of the quaking was revealed when the alien Terramole burst up through the ground, roaring in triumph. "Lothor has unleashed me!" he cried. "Now Earth is ours!"

As the Yellow Ranger plunged himself deep into the ground, his fellow Rangers called out: "Wait, Dustin! You can't battle Terramole by yourself!" "Remember our training—to work as a team!"

"I can handle this alone!" Dustin called back.
The Yellow Ranger burst up through the rocks, surprising the alien. But even his Ninja skills and earth powers were no match for this fierce enemy.

"Prepare to bite the dust!" roared Terramole. "I am stronger than any one of you Rangers!"

"But not if we three work as one!" cried the Blue Ranger. "Come on, Shane! Let's show this dirtbag some real Ranger spirit! Sonic Fin! Sound off!"
"Hawk Blaster! Fired up!"
"Lion Hammer! Ready to roar!"

Lothor watched in anger. "I wanted to split them up! I knew the Yellow Ranger would try to defeat Terramole by himself. But now those other two have joined him!"

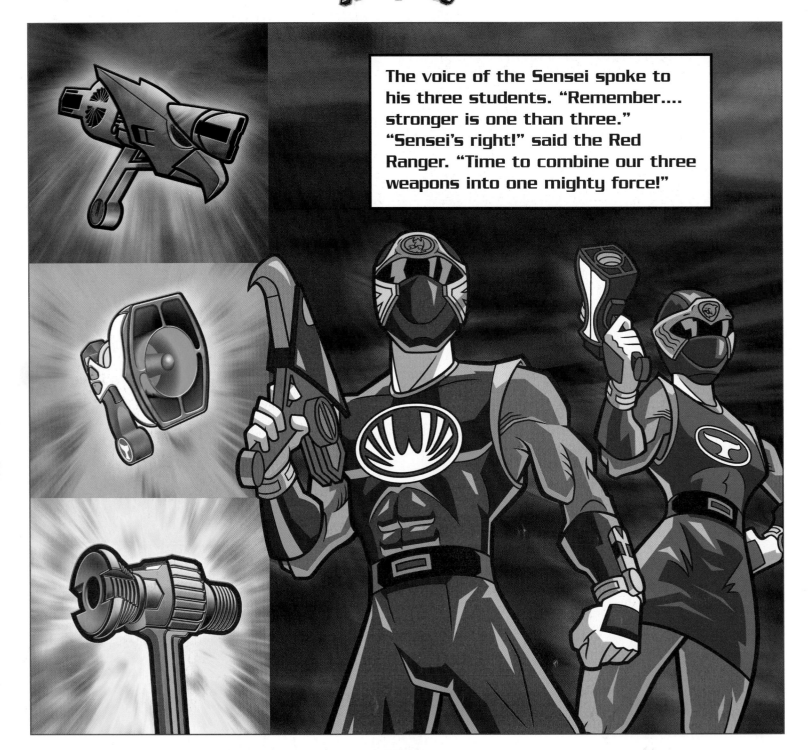

The voice of the Sensei spoke to his three students. "Remember.... stronger is one than three." "Sensei's right!" said the Red Ranger. "Time to combine our three weapons into one mighty force!"

"Storm Striker!" the three cried. With one blast from the Storm Striker, it was Terramole who bit the dust!

"Scroll of Empowerment! Descend!" ordered Lothor.
Suddenly, Terramole reappeared—as a giant!
"No way!" said Shane. "We're going to need some help with this guy."
"Big time help," agreed Tori.

"I am sending the Zords," came Sensei's words. "You will pilot these powerful robotic vehicles. For Shane—the Red Hawk Zord. For Tori—the Blue Dolphin Zord. For Dustin—the Yellow Lion Zord."

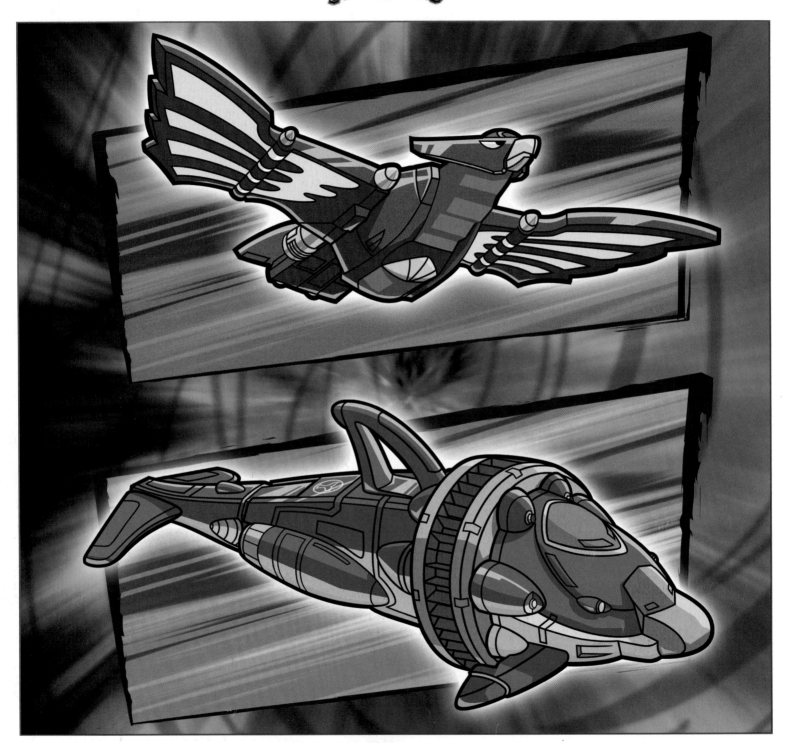

"Let's fight fire with fire!" called Shane, blinding Terramole in a trail of flames.

"Surf's up! And you are so washed up!" said Tori, sending a tidal wave over the monster.

But Terramole stood his ground!

"I can handle this!" cried Dustin. "Lion Tornado blast!"

"Good job, bro!" said Shane. "But—oh, no! It can't be! He's still standing!"

"You cannot defeat as three," said the Sensei. "Use the force that is within you to combine your powers."

"We've got to combine our Zords," said Dustin.
With the cry of "Megazord!" the three Zords became one giant robot!

"Activate power sphere," commanded Tori.
Terramole was outmatched. With one mighty power surge from the Megazord, he was grounded—for good!
"Way cool!" cheered Dustin.

"Nice teamwork, guys," said Shane.
"Yes," said the voice of the Sensei, "and you will need this team strength when Lothor tries again to conquer Earth. However, now that you have learned to work as one, the balance of power will always be on your side."

RED LION ROAR

This is Animarium—the great floating island, home of Princess Shayla and the Wild Zords, guardians of the power of good.

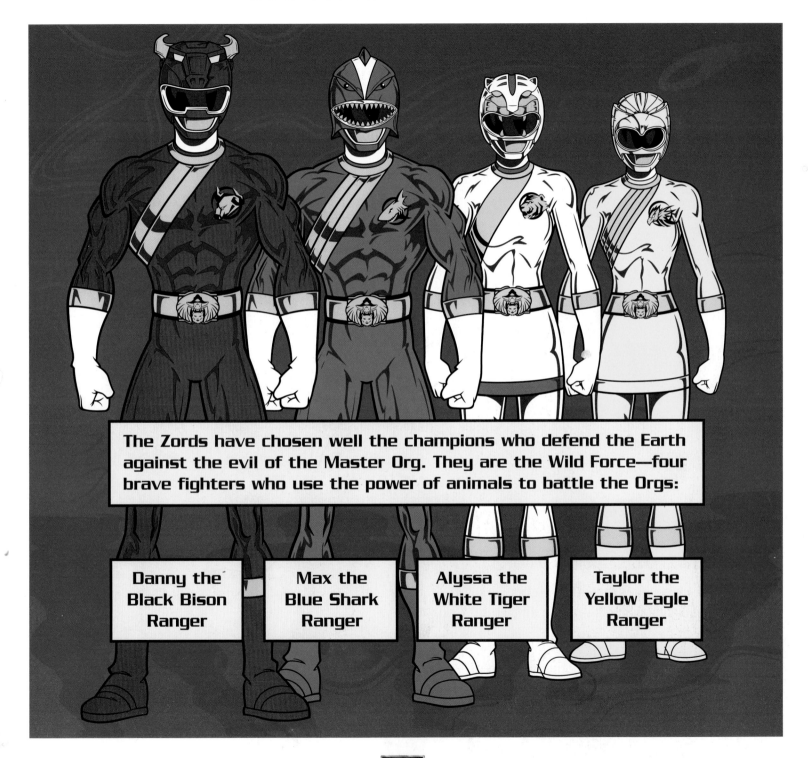

The Zords have chosen well the champions who defend the Earth against the evil of the Master Org. They are the Wild Force—four brave fighters who use the power of animals to battle the Orgs:

Danny the Black Bison Ranger

Max the Blue Shark Ranger

Alyssa the White Tiger Ranger

Taylor the Yellow Eagle Ranger

But a blast of electricity from the Turbine Org stopped them in their tracks! The force was too strong for the four Rangers to withstand.

"Princess Shayla said we needed a fifth Ranger," called out Alyssa. "She was right!"

Back in Animarium, Princess Shayla touched her jeweled neckpiece and spoke to the Rangers.

"Rangers, I have found the fifth Ranger. His name is Cole. He has been transported here to Animarium for training. I will send him to join you."

Cole had awakened to a new, amazing world. An Eagle's cry filled the air, and great Animal Zords appeared before him.

"What are you?" asked Cole.
The Lion Zord spoke to Cole's mind. "We have been searching for you. From now on, you will be the Red Ranger—with the heart of a Lion. You will help defend the earth against the evil Orgs."

Back in the city, people fled from the Turbine and Plugma Orgs. "Earth belongs to us Orgs!" cried Turbine Org as he fired his sparks around the city. Little did the Org know that the Wild Force had become a team of five....

"It is now time to find out if the Lion chose the right person," said Taylor.

"Just tell me what to do," replied Cole. The four Rangers pulled out their phones—and handed one to Cole.
"Wild access!"
"Wild access!" repeated Cole.
The five morphed into the Wild Force Rangers!

"Let's finish off those Orgs!" commanded Danny.

Cole leaped in to help his fellow Ranger. "I think I like this!" he thought. But just then, the Orgs joined arms and sent a powerful energy blast that hurled the Rangers into the air.

"Listen to me!" cried Cole. "My Lion patch is telling me that only one can defeat two! I think we have to combine our weapons and work together!"

"Let's do it!" said the Black Bison.
The five Rangers pulled out their weapons—
"Red Lion Fang!"
"Golden Eagle Sword!"
"Blue Shark Fighting Fins!"
"Black Bison Axe!"
"White Tiger Baton!"
—to form the Wild Force Jungle Sword!

The Orgs were alarmed! "I think we need another Org," moaned Turbine Org.

"Jungle Sword, strike!" roared the Red Lion.

As the Sword's mighty beam turned Plugma into a mound of slime, Turbine Org limped to safety and met up with Jindrax and Toxica. "We have a way to help you," said Toxica. With her evil powers, she turned the Org into a Giant Turbine!

"Oh, no! It's impossible!" cried the White Ranger. "Man, that is big!" said the Black Ranger. "The world is mine!" laughed Giant Turbine Org.

From Animarium, Princess Shayla sent a message: "Rangers, the time has come. Put your crystals in your Crystal Sabers and call the Wild Zords down from Animarium!"

The Rangers inserted their crystals and held their sabers high— summoning the Wild Zords! "Now, Org, you'll feel the full power of the Wild Force!" roared Cole. The Zords attacked Giant Turbine. The monster was stunned— but not stopped!

Cole refused to give up. "Wait! Remember how we beat the first Org? By working as one! We can do it again! Let's draw our weapons as one! Guardians of the Earth, united we roar!"

The Rangers held their weapons toward the Giant Turbine and proclaimed: "Wild Force—Mega-Roar!"

Beams of powerful energy shot out and joined energy beams from the Animal Zords. The incredible blast hit Giant Turbine Org—destroying him—forever!

"We did it!" yelled the Red Ranger. "*You* did it, Red," said the Blue Ranger proudly.

That night, Jindrax and Toxica cowered together in the shadows.

"My Org! My poor, poor Org..." wailed Jindrax.

"Don't worry, Jindrax," hissed Toxica. "We know the Master Org will return."

"The Master!" cried Jindrax. "We must find the Master."

The Rangers were proud of their victory, and together they congratulated their new champion—Cole, the Red Lion Ranger.

Taylor smiled and said, "Not bad for a rookie."

It is the year 3000. Ransik, the most sinister crime boss of all time, has developed an evil scheme to go back in time and take over the world.

"We're going to thaw out the most evil criminals and take them with us back to the past. We'll be unstoppable!" Ransik laughs.

Ransik sends out Frax, his alien robot, to carry out his evil plans.

An elite team of police officers known as the Time Force uses its powers to protect people from evil. Alex, a brave young officer, is hot on Frax's trail. Alex uses a Chrono Morpher to change into the Red Time Force Ranger.

Frax uses his dangerous claw grip against the Red Ranger and the other Rangers. But he's no match for their strength and skill. With Frax captured, Ransik won't be able to carry out his evil time-travel plan.

Ransik is captured by the Time Force Power Rangers team. They are called on to transport Ransik to prison, where he will be cryogenically frozen.

"That's the last we'll see of him!" says Katie, the Yellow Ranger.

"Let's put that creep into a deep freeze where he belongs!" says Lucas, the Blue Ranger.

But Ransik's Cyclobots have other plans. They ambush the transport vehicle. Ransik has escaped again!

"With an army of mutants at my side, no one in the past will be able to stop me!" Ransik laughs.

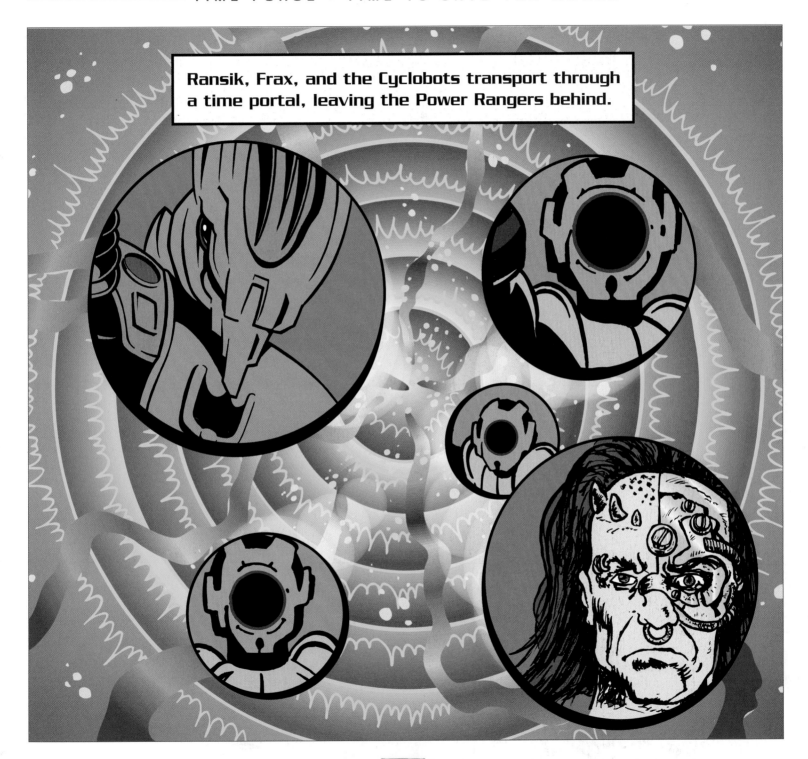

Ransik, Frax, and the Cyclobots transport through a time portal, leaving the Power Rangers behind.

Jen, the Pink Ranger, gathers her team. "We have to stop Ransik before he destroys our past... and our future," she says.

"But they could be anywhere in time!" says Trip, the Green Ranger.

"We'll just keep searching until we find them," says the Yellow Ranger.

"Let's go!" says the Blue Ranger.

The Rangers take five Chrono Morphers and step into the Time Warp. It is a strange trip, unlike anything they have ever experienced before. They do not know where they will land.

The Green Ranger suggests they might end up meeting fierce samurais.

The Yellow Ranger thinks they might come face-to-face with man-eating dinosaurs!

The Rangers land on the street in the year 2001. They see real cars for the first time! Everything is very strange to them. But one thing hasn't changed — Ransik and his evil followers are up to their old tricks!

Ransik is terrorizing the city. The Time Force Rangers fight with all their power, but the Cyclobots and Frax are very strong.

Ransik laughs. "This city is ours!"

"Not if we can help it!" shouts the Blue Ranger.

"We need help!" says the Yellow Ranger. Just when things seem to be at their absolute worst, the mysterious Quantum Ranger appears!

All of the Time Force Power Rangers join forces with the Quantum Ranger to defeat Ransik and his army.

"We need the Megazords!" shouts the Yellow Ranger. The Green Ranger uses his Chrono Morpher to talk to Circuit, who sends the Time Flyers back from the future. The Rangers unite to form the Megazords!

Ransik and his evil mutants are no match for the Megazords. By working together as a team, the Rangers are able to save the city.

Ransik will travel through time again, but he'll always have the Time Force Power Rangers following his every move!

Destructive forces were at work in the universe. The evil Lothor, dark twin of the wise Ninja Master Sensei, sought to conquer and control the Earth. But every plan failed—because of three brave teens.

These were the Wind Ninja Power Rangers, trained by the Sensei himself. Even Lothor's own Thunder Ninja Rangers deserted him to join the force of good. For this, Lothor blamed his bumbling officer, Choobo.

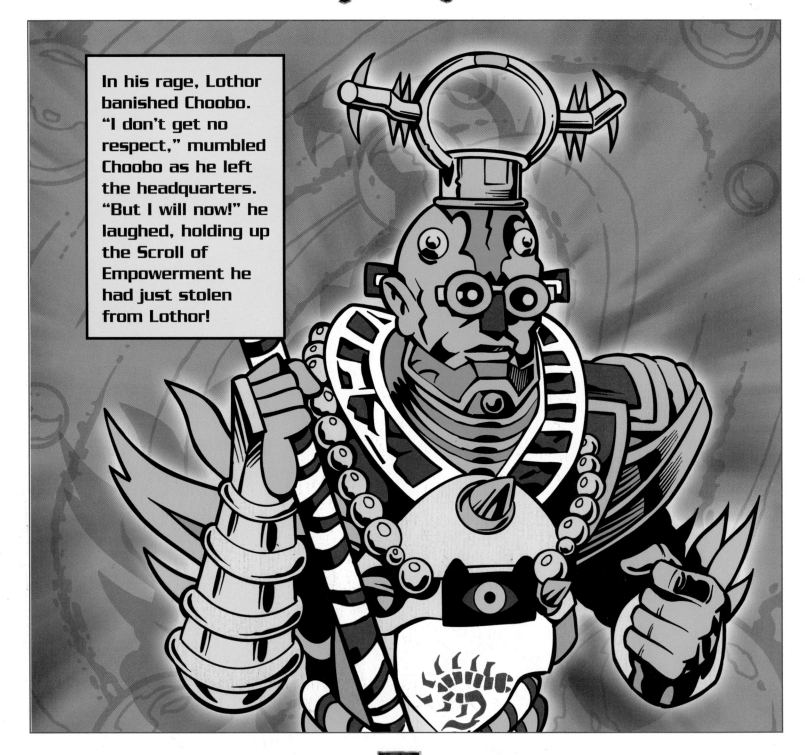

In his rage, Lothor banished Choobo. "I don't get no respect," mumbled Choobo as he left the headquarters. "But I will now!" he laughed, holding up the Scroll of Empowerment he had just stolen from Lothor!

"Now I, Choobo, will capture the Crimson and Navy Thunder Rangers—and bend them to my will. Then the three Wind Rangers will destroy them! I will be honored and respected!"

Through trickery, Choobo captured the unsuspecting brothers, Hunter and Blake, and placed them under his alter-dimensional control.

"Ha-ha!" cried Choobo. "And now I will wait for those three pesky teens to come looking for their friends. Wait till they see how the Thunder Rangers have returned to the dark force! Ha-ha!"

The voice of the Ninja Sensei spoke to his three students. "The Crimson and Navy Thunder Rangers have been captured by Choobo. Only you can rescue them."
At once the three heroes called out, "Ninja Storm! Ranger Form!"
They morphed into the Wind Power Rangers:
Shane, the Red Ranger, with the power of air.
Tori, the Blue Ranger, with the power of water.
Dustin, the Yellow Ranger, with the power of earth.

"Hand over our comrades, Choobo!" cried Shane as they landed their Ranger Gliders and confronted the cowering alien.

"They have joined with me to destroy the Earth!" Choobo cried back. "You'll have to destroy *them* if you want to save your precious Earth! Ha-ha!"

"Forget it, dude," said Dustin. "There's no way we're believing that about our fellow Rangers." "Yeah!" agreed Tori. "They used to be Lothor's, but that's water under the bridge. Prepare to surrender!"

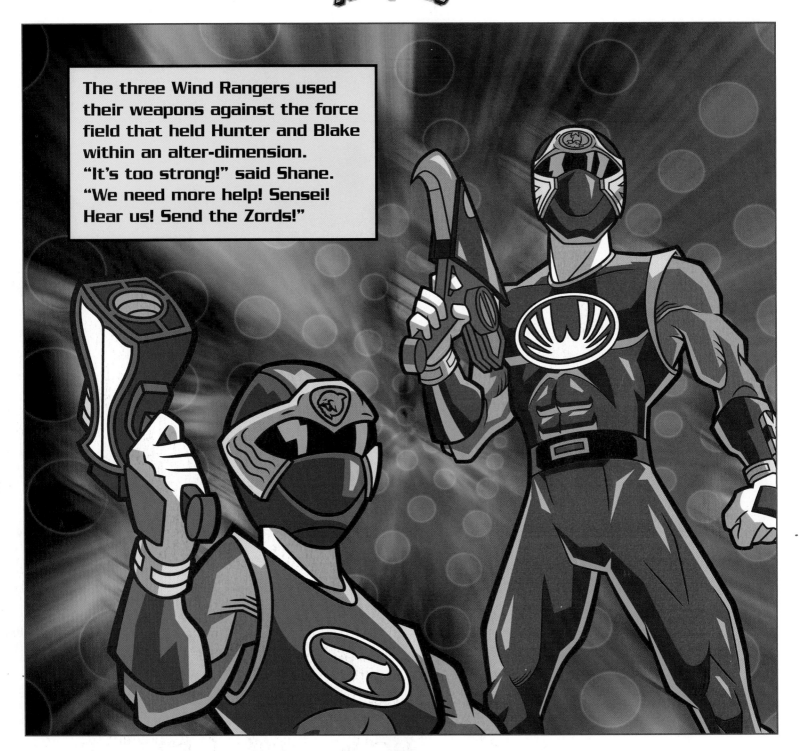

The three Wind Rangers used their weapons against the force field that held Hunter and Blake within an alter-dimension. "It's too strong!" said Shane. "We need more help! Sensei! Hear us! Send the Zords!"

Choobo watched in fear as the Red Hawk Zord, the Blue Dolphin Zord, and the Yellow Lion Zord appeared. With a fiery blast, a crushing wave, and a monstrous tornado, the three Zords broke the power that held the two Thunder Rangers.

"Great work!" said Hunter, the Crimson Ranger. "Now, let's kick this Choobo chump outta here!"

"You fools!" sneered Choobo. "I can fight five as easily as three! Scroll of Empowerment— do my bidding!"

With a flash of light, Choobo became gigantic! He swatted the Hawk Zord out of the way as he strode toward the Lion Zord to crush it beneath his huge feet.

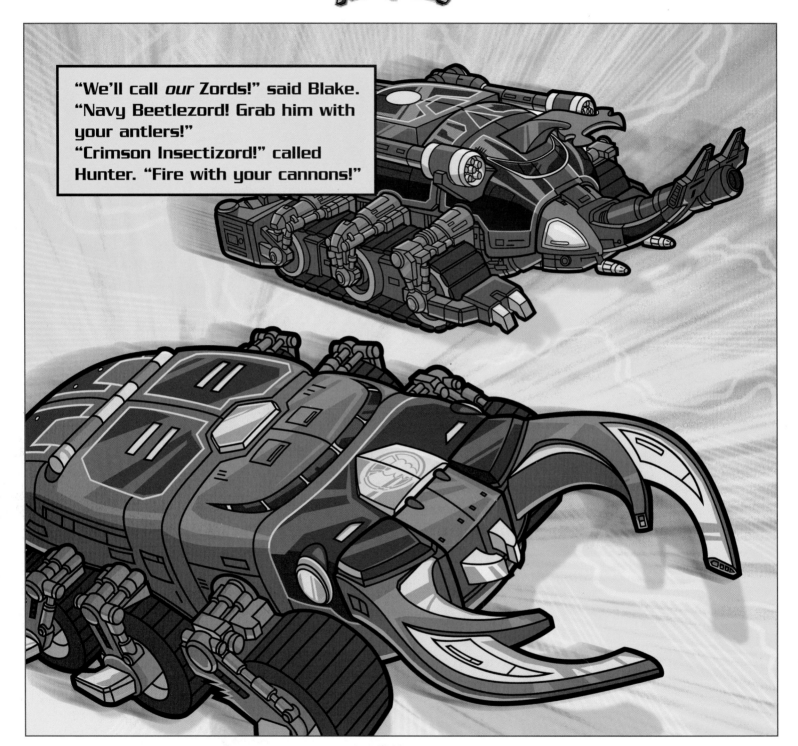

"We'll call *our* Zords!" said Blake. "Navy Beetlezord! Grab him with your antlers!"
"Crimson Insectizord!" called Hunter. "Fire with your cannons!"

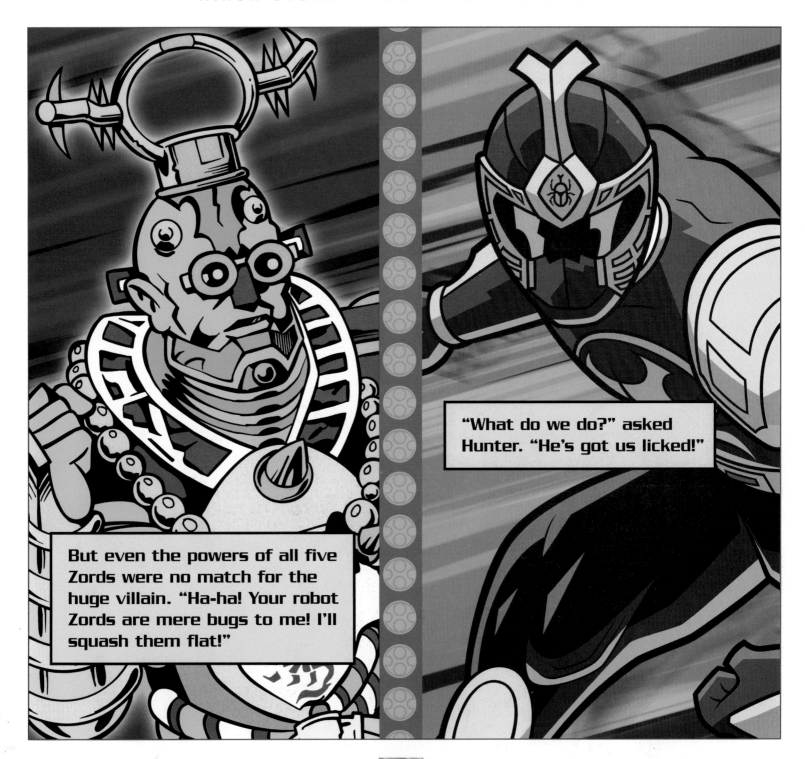

But even the powers of all five Zords were no match for the huge villain. "Ha-ha! Your robot Zords are mere bugs to me! I'll squash them flat!"

"What do we do?" asked Hunter. "He's got us licked!"

"No, bro, he doesn't," said Shane. "If you two want to be Power Rangers, you've got to start acting—and thinking—like Power Rangers. And that means thinking like a team—a team of five."

"Are you thinking what I'm thinking?" asked Tori.

"Totally!" answered Dustin.

"Totally what?" asked Blake, giving Hunter a puzzled look.

"Totally Megazord to the max!" cried Dustin. "Let's do it, Rangers! Thunder Zords and Storm Zords—to the fifth power!"

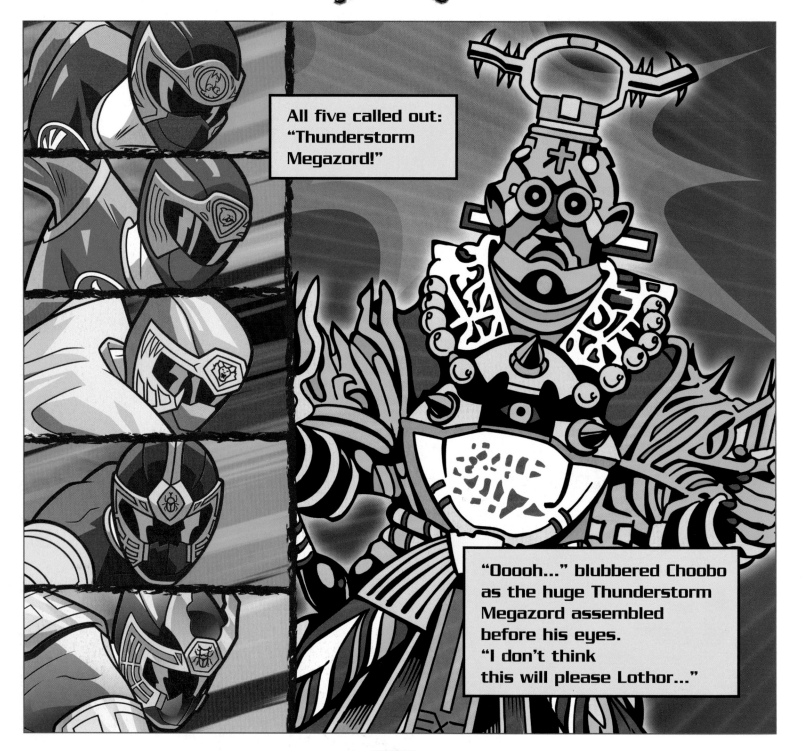

All five called out: "Thunderstorm Megazord!"

"Ooooh..." blubbered Choobo as the huge Thunderstorm Megazord assembled before his eyes. "I don't think this will please Lothor..."

The five teens high-fived to their success.
"Nothing like a good team," said Dustin.
"So... we *are* on the team now?" asked Hunter.
"You bet, dudes," answered Shane.
"For sure," said Tori.
"Way cool!" cheered Blake.

No one believes reports of a haunted temple in Turtle Cove; but Max, the Blue Ranger, thinks it's an Org.

Following up on his hunch, Max discovers the Bell Org at the temple and morphs. "Wild Access!"

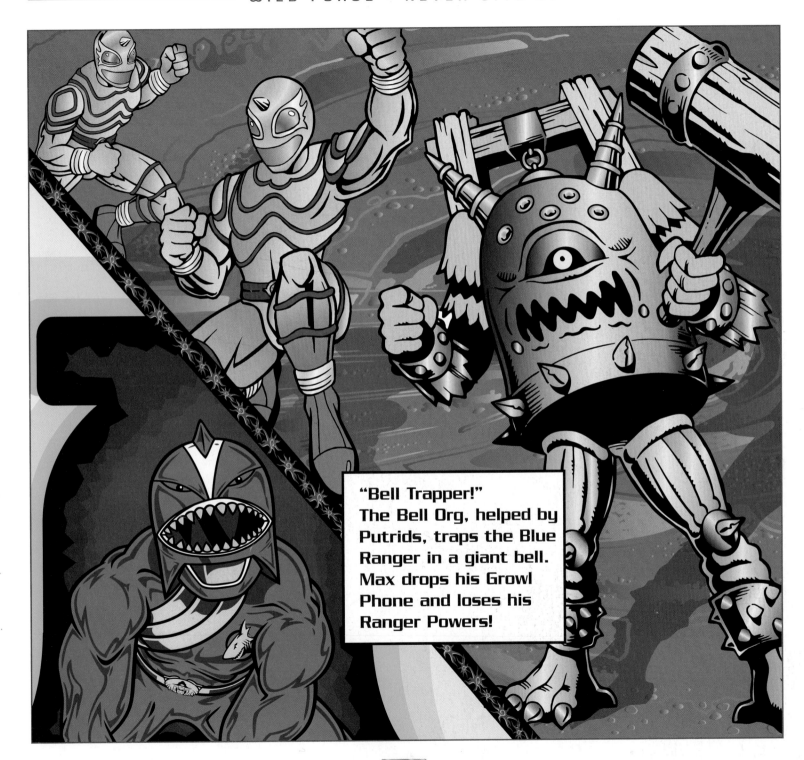

"Bell Trapper!"
The Bell Org, helped by Putrids, traps the Blue Ranger in a giant bell. Max drops his Growl Phone and loses his Ranger Powers!

Princess Shayla alerts the Rangers about the Bell Org and they take off to help Max.

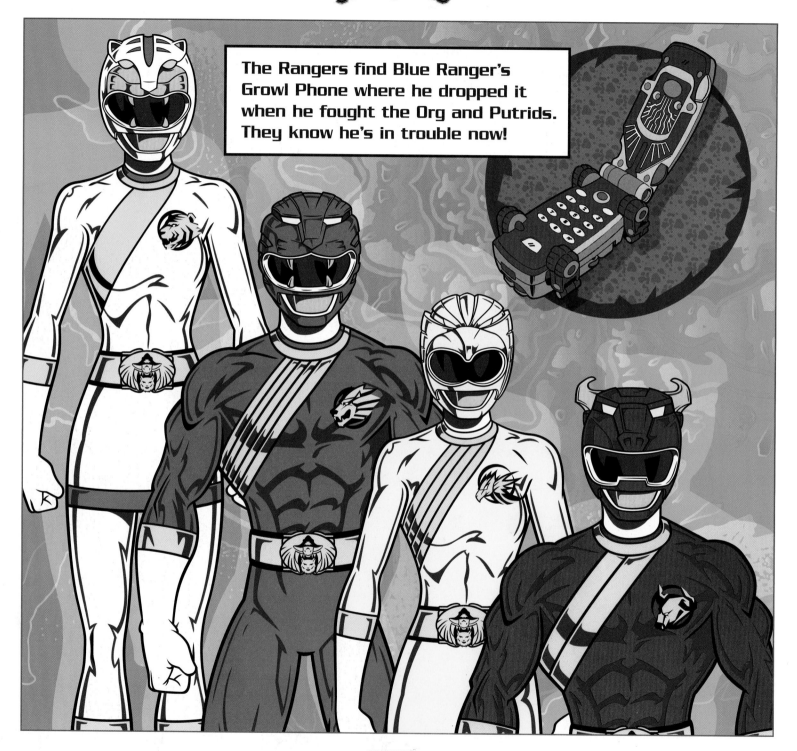

The Rangers find Blue Ranger's Growl Phone where he dropped it when he fought the Org and Putrids. They know he's in trouble now!

Jindrax and Toxica appear with a gang of Putrids to try to stop the Rangers from rescuing their friend. The fight is on!

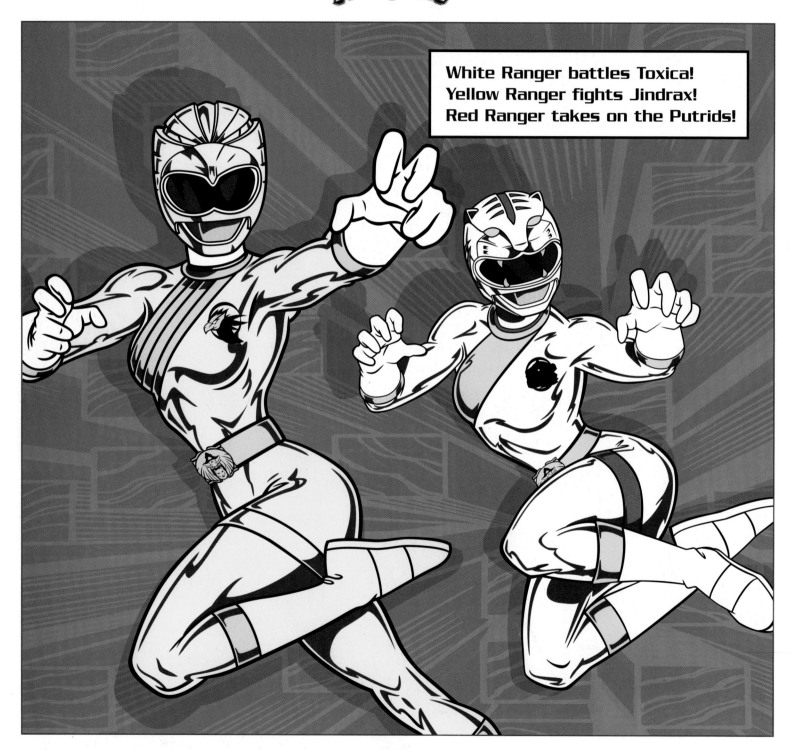

White Ranger battles Toxica!
Yellow Ranger fights Jindrax!
Red Ranger takes on the Putrids!

Meanwhile, the Black Ranger faces off against the Bell Org as he calls for his friend, Max, the Blue Ranger. Then he hears Max, trapped under a bell on the cliff!

"Never give up!" Danny calls out to Max, as he climbs the cliff.

Max hears Danny coming to save him, but then the Bell Org blasts the Black Ranger!

The Black Ranger keeps climbing as the Blue Ranger gains strength. "Never give up!"

Aided by the powers of the Shark and Bison, Danny blasts the bell open to release Max. The team reunites: "Guardians of the Earth, United We Roar!"

Danny and Max team up to battle the Bell Org together.

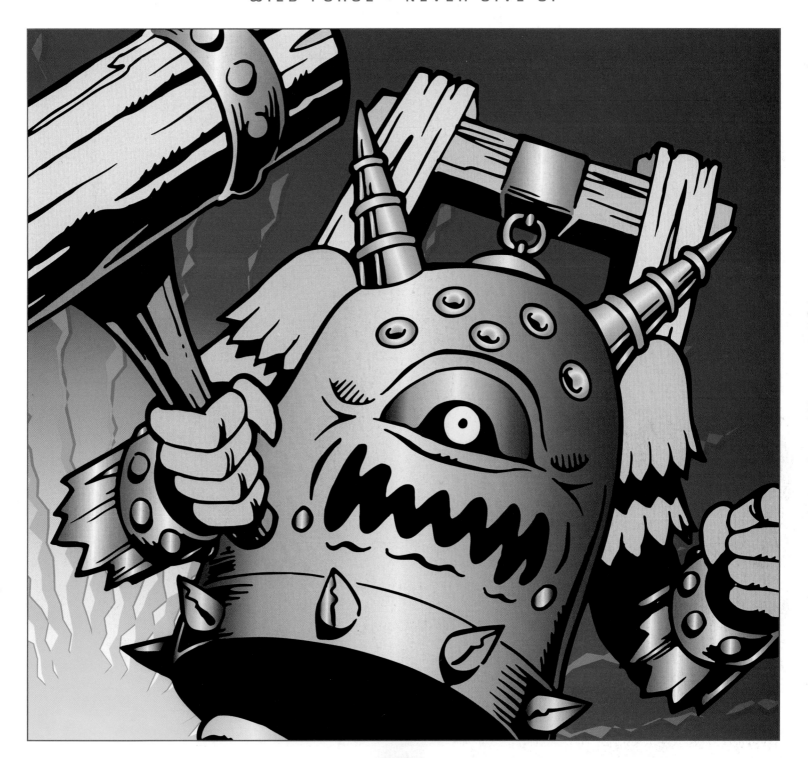

The Rangers combine their weapons to form the Jungle Sword and defeat the Bell Org.

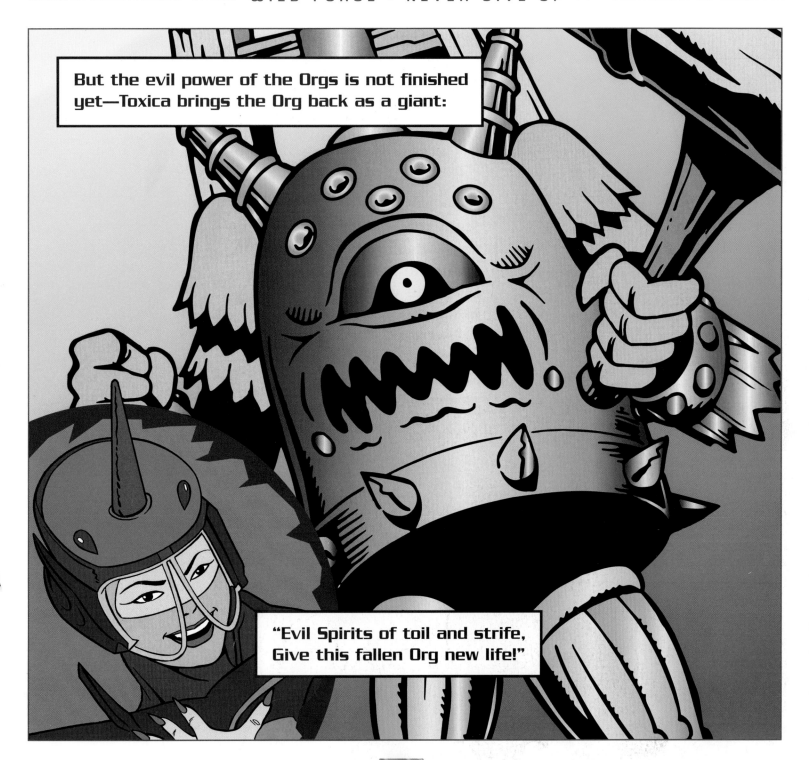

But the evil power of the Orgs is not finished yet—Toxica brings the Org back as a giant:

"Evil Spirits of toil and strife, Give this fallen Org new life!"

Then the Rangers call the Wild Zords from Animarium. There is only one way the Rangers can fight this Org—Eagle, Tiger, Bison, Lion and Shark join together:

Things still look bad for Animarium until the Black Ranger calls for the Megazord's Bison Kick. The Megazord kicks the Bell Trapper back at the Org, trapping him!

Trapped in his own bell, the Org is destroyed by one final Mega Roar laser blast from the Rangers' Megazord. He's toast!

Together, the Rangers will never give up.

Lucas
&
Luray